Eddie and the Zedlines

by

Colin Dowland

Illustrated by Phillip Morrison

To all my pupils past and present
Even those who were unpleasant

First published in Great Britain by Barrington Stoke Ltd
10 Belford Terrace, Edinburgh, EH4 3DQ
Copyright © 1999 Colin Dowland
Illustrations © Phillip Morrison
The moral right of the author has been asserted in
accordance with the Copyright, Designs and
Patents Act 1988
ISBN 1-902260-31-7
Printed by Polestar AUP Aberdeen Ltd

MEET THE AUTHOR - COLIN DOWLAND

What is your favourite animal?
The armadillo
What is your favourite boy's name?
Anything but Colin!
What is your favourite girl's name?
Her name is Ann
What is your favourite food?
Smelly cheese
What is your favourite music?
Jazz, classical or corny
What is your favourite hobby?
D.I.Y.

MEET THE ILLUSTRATOR - PHILLIP MORRISON

What is your favourite animal?
My Rhodesian Ridgeback dog, Malone
What is your favourite boy's name?
Jack
What is your favourite girl's name?
Sasha
What is your favourite food?
Seafood
What is your favourite music?
The Beach Boys
What is your favourite hobby?
Surfing

Barrington Stoke was a famous and much-loved story-teller. He travelled from village to village carrying a lantern to light his way. He arrived as it grew dark and when the young boys and girls of the village saw the glow of his lantern, they hurried to the central meeting place. They were full of excitement and expectation, for his stories were always wonderful.

Then Barrington Stoke set down his lantern. In the flickering light the listeners were enthralled by his tales of adventure, horror and mystery. He knew exactly what they liked best and he loved telling a good story. And another. And then another. When the lantern burned low and dawn was nearly breaking, he slipped away. He was gone by morning, only to appear the next day in some other village to tell the next story.

Contents

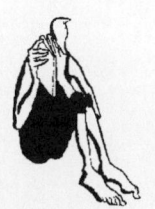

Chapter 1
The Zedroom

Eddie found himself lying face down on a stone-cold floor. It was dark and he was confused. Something had happened to him, but he wasn't sure what.

One thing he was sure about. He had a splitting headache. Putting his hand up to the back of his head, Eddie felt a sticky wet patch. He was bleeding.

Eddie struggled dizzily to his feet and dusted down his school blazer. Then it all came back to him.

He was at school, up in the Zedroom at the top of the clocktower. This was where Eddie had spent almost every lunchtime for the past two terms. It was the home of *The Zedlines* – the St Zack's school newspaper.

He remembered staying after school to start clearing out the Zedroom. He had stumbled across a report he had been writing about some computers that had been stolen from a nearby school. Then he remembered starting to pick up the rubbish from the Zedroom floor. After this, his mind went blank.

Eddie looked beside him in the gloom. There was the old, inky printer with its operating handle sticking out to the side. He must have hit his head on the stupid handle as he stood up and knocked himself out!

Eddie fumbled in the darkness looking for the door. Finding it at last, he turned the handle and pushed hard. The door didn't budge. He turned the handle again and pushed even harder. It was no good.

Eddie reached up to turn on the lights, but couldn't find the switch. It was on the outside of the door. The caretaker had locked him in. He moved to the window and held up his watch to read it from the moonlight.

"Holy pants," Eddie gasped.

It was five past six. He should have been home over two hours ago. His Mum would be worried sick.

Eddie began to panic. He had heard the stories of a ghost in the clocktower. It was said that a pupil had thrown herself out of the window after doing badly in her exams. The thought sent a shudder racing through his bones.

Eddie pushed the window open and leaned out as far as he could.

"Help ... help ...!!" he shouted. "I'm locked in. Up in the tower. Someone help me ...!"

Eddie listened, but all he could hear was the echo of his own shaky voice booming around the school buildings. An empty coke can rolled noisily across the playground. The caretaker's house was around the other side of the school. No one would hear him calling. He would be trapped up at the top of the haunted tower all night. He pulled the collar of his jacket up around his neck and shivered.

"This place is always so untidy," said a strange voice from out of the darkness.

Chapter 2
Ghost Writers

Eddie froze. His heart began to thump wildly and a cold sweat broke out onto his skin.

"Who ... who's there?" Eddie said, his voice weak and trembling.

"It's just terrible," groaned the strange voice again after a moment's silence.

Eddie shuffled backwards towards the door and put out his arms to protect himself. His eyes darted around the room, straining to see into the darkness.

There was a click and a whirr that made Eddie jump backwards. At the far end of the room, the Zedroom computer buzzed into life. The light from the screen filled the room with a bright grey glow. Eddie looked left and right and was ready to scream. But there was nobody to be seen.

In front of him was the long table where Eddie and his friends sat down to plan each newspaper. It was littered with pictures, bits of newspapers and scribbled notes. A large mug of pens, pencils and other writing equipment stood in the middle. Shelves of old books lined one wall, mostly picked up at jumble sales or given away by the school library. Everything looked normal.

There was a rustle of papers from the middle of the table. Eddie backed away thinking it might be a mouse or a rat. He pulled a large book from the shelf and held it up as a weapon.

The rustling grew stronger and then from underneath the papers crawled a strange mass of black and white squares.

"It's left like this every day. It's an utter disgrace," grunted the mass of squares.

Eddie blinked and shook his head. *Was he seeing things?*

"And it's your fault," it continued, jabbing with the corner of a white square in the direction of Eddie.

It then started to move the pieces of paper across the table, putting them into some kind of order.

"Kids of today," it muttered. "They've no standards."

Eddie was speechless. Perhaps the bang to his head had done some serious damage.

"Don't take any notice, old chap," said a rather posh voice from under Eddie's nose. "He's always like that."

The thick book that Eddie was holding leapt from his grasp and landed on the table with a thud.

"Shonnery's the name," said the book "Dick Shonnery. Licensed to spell."

Eddie gulped. "Er ... hello."

"You don't need to take any notice of Crossword over there, old boy," said Dick. He pointed one of his pages in the direction of the mass of black and white squares. "He hasn't a nice word to say about anyone. He's never happy. Always cross. Such is the life of a crossword."

"Oh, go and check your spellings, know-it-all!" snapped the Crossword.

"Now," said Dick to Eddie. "Who are you and what are … ?"

"Excuse me," interrupted Crossword rather rudely. "I ask the questions around here." The crossword shifted its squares and cleared its throat. "Three down and four across – Who are you and what are you doing here?"

Eddie looked around him to see if anyone was looking. He had never had a conversation with anything like this before.

"I'm Eddie," said Eddie. "I knocked myself out on the printer handle and now I've been locked in here by the caretaker."

"But," said Dick, pushing Crossword out of the way, "what the blazes were you doing up here so late?"

The crossword was about to interrupt again, but Dick Shonnery poked it between the squares and it waddled off in a huff.

"Well," said Eddie with a big sigh. "I was collecting up all my belongings. They're closing down *The Zedlines* and letting the teachers have the Zedroom for marking books."

For a second, there was a deathly silence. Then suddenly, the room went mad. There was a scream of horror from the horoscope. A pencil snapped and went crazy, drawing all over the table. A felt tip ran out, the computer crashed, paper flew in all directions and Dick Shonnery closed his pages with a loud bang.

Chapter 3
Spelling it out

"You mean," said Dick Shonnery, opening up just a little, "that it's the end of the line for *The Zedlines*?"

Eddie nodded. "Mr Fairman, our headmaster, said that there just isn't the space in the school to keep it going. There aren't any other rooms we can use either."

"I'm lost for words," said Crossword, who was looking more puzzled than cross.

One by one, the bits and pieces from the table came out from their hiding places and stood together in a group.

"It's a very sticky situation," said the pot of glue, giving himself a nervous stir.

The horoscope let out a terrible moan. "I see a dark future for us all."

"Just give me a couple of rounds with that headmaster of yours," puffed the hole-punch who was training to be a boxer. "I'll punch a few holes in him and give him what's for. Left hook, uppercut and he'll be out for the count. I can beat anyone."

"Oh do shut up, Hole-punch," snapped a rather old pair of scissors who was known for her very cutting remarks. "You couldn't beat eggs!"

"And you couldn't cut butter," said the glue-pot who stuck out his tongue.

The scissors gasped. "Go and stick it up your ..."

"Do cut it out, Scissors old thing," Dick interrupted, taking charge of the situation. "I see it this way. There are two choices. We can either sit around arguing with each other or we can stand up for our writes!"

"What do you mean?" said a rather thick notepad, with a blank look on its page.

"Well," continued Dick, who was used to spelling things out for people, "with the help of young Ed here we can put together the best ever copy of *The Zedlines*. A copy that would make *The Zedlines* just too good to close down.

There was a cheer from the desk. The bulldog clip woofed with delight and even miserable old Crossword gave a broad five letter smile.

Chapter 4
Paper Work

At once, the room was abuzz with the scratching of pens and snipping of scissors.

Crossword was building up a huge pattern of squares and was busy writing clues for himself with the help of Dick Shonnery.

The pot of glue and the scissors were carefully sorting through old copies of *The Zedlines*. They were to cut out the best and most important stories of the year. The teachers had to realise how important *The Zedlines* was to the school.

Even the horoscope was busy. She sat at the window looking up at the stars, groaning and making notes.

Meanwhile, Eddie began to search through some of the papers that littered the floor of the Zedroom.

"Gotcha," he exclaimed, holding up a piece of paper with some of his own scribbles on. It was the unfinished report about the computers that had been stolen from a nearby school. He would finish the report and he would make it his very best piece of work.

He looked around for something to write with. Most of the pens were already busy writing. A report about the school fête was nearly finished and the latest sports results from the football and netball teams were being worked out by the calculator.

The crayons and pencils meanwhile were lined up behind the sharpener.

"Excuse me," Eddie asked, feeling embarrassed, "I wonder if I might borrow one of you for a moment or two?"

Instantly, the pens and pencils ran across the table towards him and stood to attention in two rows like skinny soldiers.

"Ready for inspection, sir," bellowed one of the pencils. It adjusted the rubber on top of its head, so that it was exactly straight.

Eddie was amazed. It was a first class display. He looked down at the ranks. There were ballpoint pens, marker pens, felt tip pens and every shade of pencil lead you could wish for. Eddie couldn't decide.

"2B or not 2B? That is the question," asked a rather fine pencil, shaking its lead from side to side.

In the end, Eddie selected a short, stubby pencil. He began frantically rewriting some of the sentences from his report on the stolen computers. It had to be perfect.

For the next hour, Eddie was so involved in his writing that he forgot to think about how late home he was. He forgot about his headache too. He didn't even mind being locked inside the haunted tower. Putting together *The Zedlines* each month was what Eddie loved to do most.

He and a few friends had started it after a newspaper project at school. The name was Eddie's idea. St Zack's pupils were nicknamed Zedheads by pupils from a nearby school. He combined 'Zedheads' with 'headlines' and came up with *The Zedlines*. After that the Zedroom was the obvious name for the editing room of the newspaper. It had started with just one page, but now ran to four pages with news, sports results, a crossword and a fake horoscope.

The thought of *The Zedlines* closing down was just terrible. If the teachers didn't give them so much work to do, they wouldn't need a stupid room for marking books.

At last, Eddie put down the pencil he was using.

"I'm worn out," it said rather bluntly and hobbled away to get resharpened.

Eddie's report was ready for typing up. He went over to the old computer and sat down. A

message flashed up on the screen in front of him.

EVENING ALL.

P.C. 8256 AT YOUR SERVICE.

YOUR COMMAND IS MY WORD.

PLEASE TYPE IN YOUR REPORT EDDIE.

But before he had put finger to key, a light flickered across the ceiling of the Zedroom. The sound of a car engine could be heard in the playground below.

'ALLO, 'ALLO, 'ALLO, displayed P.C. 8256.
WHAT'S GOING ON HERE, THEN?

Chapter 5
A Man and a Plan

Eddie dashed to the window. It had to be somebody coming to rescue him.

He leaned out as far as he could and was about to shout down when he heard the sound of glass being smashed.

Across the playground below, Eddie could just make out the figure of a man. He was dressed in dark clothes and carrying a torch.

His arm was reaching through a broken window
in the door that led from the playground into
the computer room. A small van was backed up
close by with its back doors wide open.

Dick Shonnery flapped his pages and flew
across to the windowsill.

"What is it, Ed, old boy?" he said.

Eddie had realised instantly what was going on. He moved away from the window and back to the table.

"It's what I've been writing about in my report," said Eddie, pointing to the piece of paper that he had left next to the computer. "Someone's going to try and steal the computers from St Zack's too."

Eddie began to pace up and down the room.

"I have to do something," he said. "But what can I do stuck up here?"

A ripple of conversation spread around the Zedliners as they discussed what could be done. Then, there was a loud slap on the table from the metre ruler. Everyone went quiet.

The ruler stood up on its end and began to speak. "My fellow Zedliners. As chosen ruler of this desk of ours, I will come straight to the

point. Young Master Eddie here has been trying to help save *The Zedlines* for us. Therefore, we shouldn't just remain stationary, Stationery. We should try and help him in return."

"He's jolly well right," agreed Dick. "Gather round, pen pals. I think I've got an idea."

The Zedliners huddled together and Dick Shonnery spelled out what they had to do.

*****

When everyone was quite sure of the plan, there was a quiet roll from the drum of the old, inky printer.

On the sound of the drum, the pencils collected together and stood to attention in one row. In the next row, the crayons had lined themselves up into the correct rainbow order according to shade. The pens found their tops and stood behind the crayons. The other assorted Zedliners formed a fourth row. At the back of the group was the hole-punch who was happily shadow-boxing all on his own.

The roll from the inky printer stopped and began to take on a more regular beat.

At the front of the group stood a tall, permanent marker pen who was marking time with its nib by swaying from side to side. It stood to attention and turned to the rest of the Zedliners.

"By the write ... quick march," it bellowed.

The troop of Zedliners marched forwards towards the window in time to the drum. Crossword waddled along at the back without a clue, trying to keep up and moaning all the time.

Approaching the edge of the long table, the ruler ran ahead. Slowly and carefully, it laid itself down flat to bridge the gap between the table and the windowsill.

"Left, write, left, write," boomed the marker pen.

At double quick time, the troop of Zedliners marched across the bridge that the ruler had made. Once across, the writing troops lined themselves up in front of the window.

"Stationery ... halt!" commanded the marker pen.

"You all know what to do," said Dick Shonnery grinning from A to Z. "Good luck everyone. Go to it, Zedliners."

Chapter 6
Into Action

In an instant, the regimented lines of the pens and pencils broke up. The Zedliners had some serious paperwork to do.

First, the paper-clips linked arms and formed themselves into an enormous chain. One by one, they lowered themselves out of the window.

Then two staplers, loaded and ready for action, climbed into the centre pages of Dick Shonnery.

Dick checked that his pages were smooth and his jacket straight. He was ready for a spell of danger.

Down below, Eddie could see that the thief had loaded a computer into the back of his van and was going back into the school for more.

"Okay, Ed, old boy," said Dick. "I'm ready for take off. Just pick me up, drop me out of the window and stand clear."

Eddie was in no state to argue. He gently picked up the book and made sure that the staplers were still in place. Then, holding his breath, Eddie dropped it out of the window.

There was a gasp from the watching Zedliners. The pale crayons turned a shade paler and the notepad's lines felt faint.

At first Dick Shonnery fell like a stone, tumbling down towards the ground. Then, with a quick flap of his pages, the book soared back upwards, circling high up over the robber's head. Dick was ready for a dive.

As the man staggered into the playground, carrying a second computer, Dick Shonnery pinned back his pages and dived steeply towards the robber. Swooping down, just above him, the staplers opened fire sending a sharp stream of missiles at the robber's head.

Caught by surprise, the robber dropped the computer and began swatting wildly in front of his face as if attacked by a swarm of bees. As he did so, the chain of paper-clips began swinging around his head, paper-clipping him around the ear.

Back at the top of the clocktower, the sticky tape had attached itself to the window pane. Then, with a loud scream, it threw itself out of the window, unrolling noisily as it went.

Meanwhile, the ruler had lodged itself between the window and the windowsill. With the help of the hole-punch and the snarling bulldog clip, the ruler bent itself backwards as far as it could go.

The glue-pot turned to the correcting fluid. "On you get," instructed the glue-pot, pointing a sticky stirring stick at the ruler.

The correcting fluid had already unscrewed itself and taken out its brush. It shuffled onto the end of the ruler, its brush pointing forward like a sword.

The glue-pot followed, giving himself a good stir. "Stick to me and you'll be fine," cheered the glue-pot. He shook the correcting fluid firmly by the brush and then saluted.

The ruler lined itself up ready to fire its two passengers out of the window.

"I'm ready," it twanged.

"Just to the left a bit," corrected the correcting fluid.

The bulldog clip and the hole-punch nodded and started the countdown.

"Three ... two ... one ... FIRE!"

The ruler sprang forward and the glue-pot and correcting fluid flew out of the window at incredible speed.

Eddie looked down to see them catapulted towards the robber. "Up here," he shouted.

The robber, surprised by the voice, looked up towards the clocktower window. As he did so, the glue and correcting fluid hit him full in the face and he was covered in sticky white goo.

Blinded by the glue, the robber began to panic.

"I'm getting outta here," he screamed, trying to wipe his face and heading for the van door. But he hadn't allowed for the sticky tape that had all the time been wrapping itself around his feet. He took one step and fell flat on his face.

Dick Shonnery, now flying high, began his final dive. He lined up his spine, closed his pages a little and set his aim. Down he swept towards the struggling robber, speeding like a rocket. His pages flapped faster and faster until – SMACK! Dick Shonnery hit the robber right on the back of the head.

The man was sent flying forwards and fell to the ground in a heap.

High up in the tower, the pencils cheered and waved, shaking their leads and bouncing up and down on their rubbers. The pens threw their tops high into the air and cried inky tears of joy. The bulldog clip leapt from the windowsill and ran around the Zedroom, chasing its own tail.

A hail of gluey paper balls and paper aeroplanes floated down onto the robber. The pencils, who had sharpened and shaved themselves especially for the occasion, threw their shavings out of the window. Even the crossword was happy.

Eddie gave a whoop of delight. "You did it," he cried. "I can't believe it. You actually did it."

He knelt down to pat the over-excited bulldog clip on the head and to lift it back onto the windowsill. But, as he stood up ... WHACK!

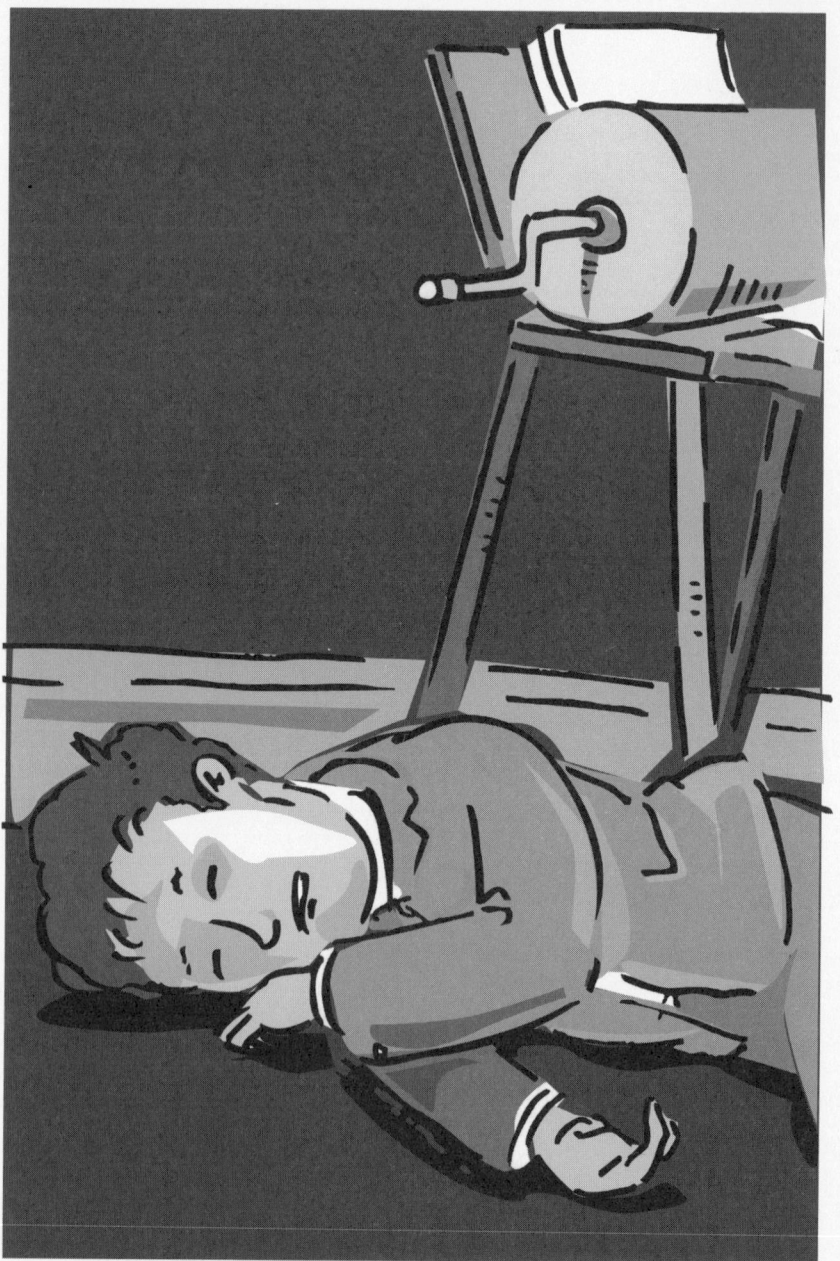

Eddie had hit his head on the operating handle of the old, inky printer again. His body slumped limp and lifeless to the floor. He was knocked out cold.

Chapter 7
Zedline News

Eddie was woken by what sounded like clanking chains. Perhaps there *was* a ghost in the clocktower after all.

The Zedroom computer was switched off and the room was back in darkness. He tried to stand up, but his head hurt even more than before.

There was a click and the striplights of the Zedroom flickered into life. Eddie shielded his eyes as they got used to the brightness. He blinked hard and could just make out the shape of the school caretaker standing at the open door rattling his big bunch of keys. A policeman stood behind him with the headmaster, Mr Fairman. Eddie could also hear the voice of his Mum calling up the clocktower stairs.

"It's all right son," said the policeman, helping Eddie to his feet. "You're safe now. And we've got the robber too."

Eddie's Mum came out from behind the policeman and wrapped Eddie in her arms, giving him a huge soppy kiss.

"I've been worried sick, Eddie. I thought something terrible had happened to you."

"I'm fine, Mum," said Eddie, wiping lipstick from his cheek. "I just hit my head a bit that's

all. The caretaker didn't know I was in here and he locked me in."

"Sorry lad," said the caretaker. "I need to be more careful next time."

"But, you're bleeding," insisted Eddie's Mum.

"Honestly, I'm fine," protested Eddie. "It's just a scratch."

The policeman stepped forward and patted Eddie warmly on the back.

"It looks like you have saved the school from losing some valuable computer equipment," he said. "It beats me how you did it from up here."

Eddie just shrugged. There was no way he could explain.

As the policeman continued, Eddie noticed a pile of newly printed copies of *The Zedlines*

that had magically appeared on the Zedroom table. Mr Fairman, his headmaster, was reading a copy. The headline read: COMPUTER THIEF BOOKED. Eddie smiled when he saw it. Dick Shonnery had booked him all right.

Mr Fairman turned to Eddie. "Is this all your own work?" he asked.

Eddie secretly crossed his fingers behind his back.

"Yes, sir," he replied.

It wasn't really a lie. Everyone had help from pens, pencils and other bits and pieces when they wrote.

"It's the very last edition," sighed Eddie sadly. "Before *The Zedlines* closes down forever."

Mr Fairman looked rather embarrassed.

"I must tell you something, Eddie," he said. "Usually, I am just too busy to read your newspaper." He held up his copy and pointed at the front page. "This report is excellent," he said excitedly. He turned to the next page. "And my horoscope is very funny. The crossword looks tricky too!"

Eddie tried not to laugh.

"I did have a *little* help ... from some pen pals of mine," he grinned.

Mr Fairman looked around at the untidy mass of papers that littered the Zedroom.

"If you could keep it tidy," he said. "I just might be able to talk the teachers into sharing this room with you. They could mark their books at lunchtimes and you could use it after school. I'm not making any promises, but I think *The Zedlines* is too good to close down."

Eddie punched the air. "Thanks sir. That's the best news ever!"

Down in the playground Eddie saw the robber being taken away by the police. He looked in a shocking state. He was covered in a crusty mixture of glue, pencil shavings and staples. Bright white correcting fluid streaked his hair and his wrists were bound together tightly with sticky tape. A chain of paper-clips hung from each ear. Some were even stuck up his nose. He really did look a sorry sight.

"So, you spent the night in the clocktower?" joked Eddie's Mum as they drove out of the school gates. "What with all those stories of it being haunted?"

Eddie looked up to the top of the clocktower.

"There's nothing up there but a few pens and pencils and books," he said. "It's not haunted. Well ... not by ghosts!"

 Other Barrington Stoke titles available:-

What's Going On, Gus? by Jill Atkins 1-902260-10-4
Nicked! by David Belbin 1-902260-29-5
Bungee Hero by Julie Bertagna 1-902260-23-6
Hostage by Malorie Blackman 1-902260-12-0
The Two Jacks by Tony Bradman 1-902260-30-9
Starship Rescue by Theresa Breslin 1-902260-24-4
Ghost for Sale by Terry Deary 1-902260-14-7
Sam the Detective by Terrance Dicks 1-902260-19-8
Billy the Squid by Colin Dowland 1-902260-04-X
Kick Back by Vivian French 1-902260-02-3
The Gingerbread House by Adèle Geras 1-902260-03-1
Danny's Great Goal by Michael Hardcastle 1-902260-32-5
Ship of Ghosts by Nigel Hinton 1-902260-33-3
Virtual Friend by Mary Hoffman 1-902260-00-7
The Genie by Mary Hooper 1-902260-20-1
Tod in Biker City by Anthony Masters 1-902260-15-5
Wartman by Michael Morpurgo 1-902260-05-8
Whirlwind by Judith O'Neill 1-902260-34-1
Extra Time by Jenny Oldfield 1-902260-13-9
Screw Loose by Alison Prince 1-902260-01-5
Life Line by Rosie Rushton 1-902260-21-X
Problems with a Python by Jeremy Strong 1-902260-22-8
Lift Off by Hazel Townson 1-902260-11-2

Barrington Stoke, 10 Belford Terrace, Edinburgh EH4 3DQ
Tel: 0131 315 4933 Fax: 0131 315 4934
E-mail: info@barringtonstoke.co.uk
Website: www.barringtonstoke.co.uk